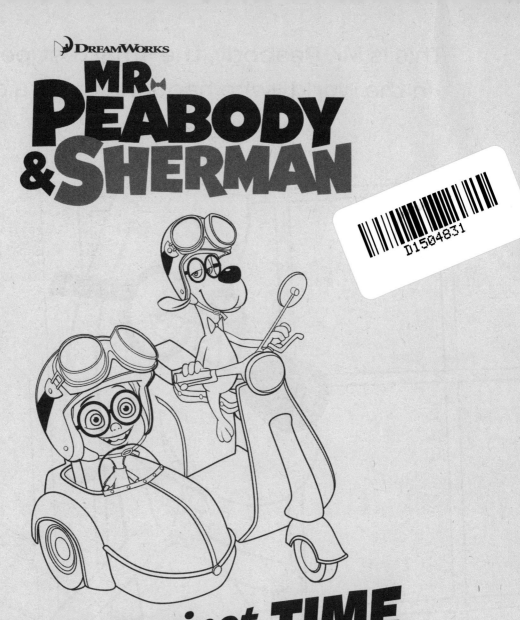

MR. PEABODY & SHERMAN

Race Against TIME

Adapted by Frank Berrios

Illustrated by Tina Francisco

A GOLDEN BOOK • NEW YORK

"Mr. Peabody & Sherman" © 2014 DreamWorks Animation L.L.C. Character rights
TM & © Ward Productions, Inc. Licensed by Bullwinkle Studios, LLC. All rights reserved.
Published in the United States by Golden Books, an imprint of Random House Children's Books,
a division of Random House LLC, 1745 Broadway,
New York, NY 10019, and in Canada by Random House of Canada Limited, Toronto,
Penguin Random House Companies. Golden Books, A Golden Book,
and the G colophon are registered trademarks of Random House LLC.
ISBN 978-0-385-37151-3
randomhouse.com/kids
Printed in the United States of America

10 9 8 7 6 5 4 3 2 1

This is Mr. Peabody, the smartest person in the world—who happens to be a dog!

How many words can you make using the letters in **PEABODY**?
Use each letter only once.

_____   _____

_____   _____

_____   _____

_____   _____

_____   _____

_____   _____

_____   _____

_____   _____

POSSIBLE ANSWERS: Ad, ape, bad, bed, body, by, dab, day, pay, pea, and pod.

How many times can you find **PEABODY** in the puzzle? Look up, down, forward, and backward.

P E A B O D Y A Y
E P E A B O D Y D
A B B D D P A E O
B Y D O B A E P B
O D Y A P E Y P A
D P Y P Y A E P E
Y D O B A E P A P

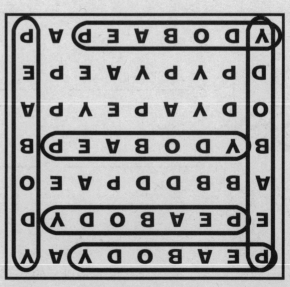

To find out the name of this boy,
cross out every **B**. Then write the remaining
letters in order on the blanks.

BBSBHBEBBRBMBABN

— — — — — — —

ANSWER: Sherman.

Sherman is Mr. Peabody's adopted son.

Mr. Peabody is a genius!
He loves teaching Sherman about history.

Count the globes.
How many are there?

Mr. Peabody invented a time-travel machine!
Use the key to find out the name of this machine.

KEY

B ___   C ___   W ___   A ___

THE ___ ___ ___ ___ ___ MACHINE

ANSWER: The WABAC machine (pronounced "way back").

Mr. Peabody and Sherman use the WABAC to go on amazing adventures!

Look at the top picture carefully. Then circle four things that are different in the bottom picture.

ANSWER:

Draw your own time-travel machine on this page.

Mr. Peabody and Sherman use the WABAC
to visit France in the eighteenth century.

Sherman meets Marie Antoinette.
She's the queen!

Design a new dress for the queen.

Circle the shadow that matches this image of Marie Antoinette.

A

B

C

Marie Antoinette likes cake—it's her favorite dessert!

Draw your favorite dessert on this page.

Count the cakes.
How many are there?

Oh, no! Mr. Peabody and Sherman must make their escape when the French Revolution begins!

Mr. Peabody and Sherman hide
in the smelly sewer. Yuck!

Help Mr. Peabody and Sherman find the WABAC machine.

ANSWER:

What is the name of this girl?
To find out, follow the lines and write each letter in the correct box.

Y N P N E

Penny thinks she is the smartest person in her class.

Sherman shares stories with his new friends.

Look at the top picture carefully. Then circle four things that are different in the bottom picture.

ANSWER:

How many times can you find **SCHOOL** in the puzzle?
Look up, down, forward, and backward.

```
L C S S L L C
L S C H O O L
O C H S O L L
O O H O H H H C
H O O C C S L
C O L S S L S
S L C H O O L
```

Why is Penny upset? To find out, start at the arrow and, going clockwise around the circle, write the letters in order on the blanks.

_ _ _ _ _ _ _ _ _ _ _ _ _

_ _ _ _ _ _ _ _ _ _!

PENNYISJEALOUSOFSHERMAN

ANSWER: Penny is jealous of Sherman!

Penny and her friends think they rule the school.

How many times can you find **PENNY** in the puzzle? Look up, down, forward, and backward.

```
Y P Y N N E P
P E N N Y P Y
Y N N E P E N
Y N N E P N N
Y Y P E N N E
P E N N Y Y P
```

How many words can you make using the letters in **SHERMAN**?
Use each letter only once.

_____   _____

_____   _____

_____   _____

_____   _____

_____   _____

_____   _____

                                _____

                                _____

                                _____

Penny teases Sherman in the lunchroom.

Penny and Sherman get into a fight!

The principal wants to talk to Mr. Peabody about Sherman.

Mean Ms. Grunion wants to take Sherman away from Mr. Peabody!

After a long day, Mr. Peabody
tucks Sherman into bed.

Mr. Peabody has a brilliant idea!

Mr. Peabody invites Penny's family over for dinner.

Circle the shadow that matches this image of Mr. Peabody.

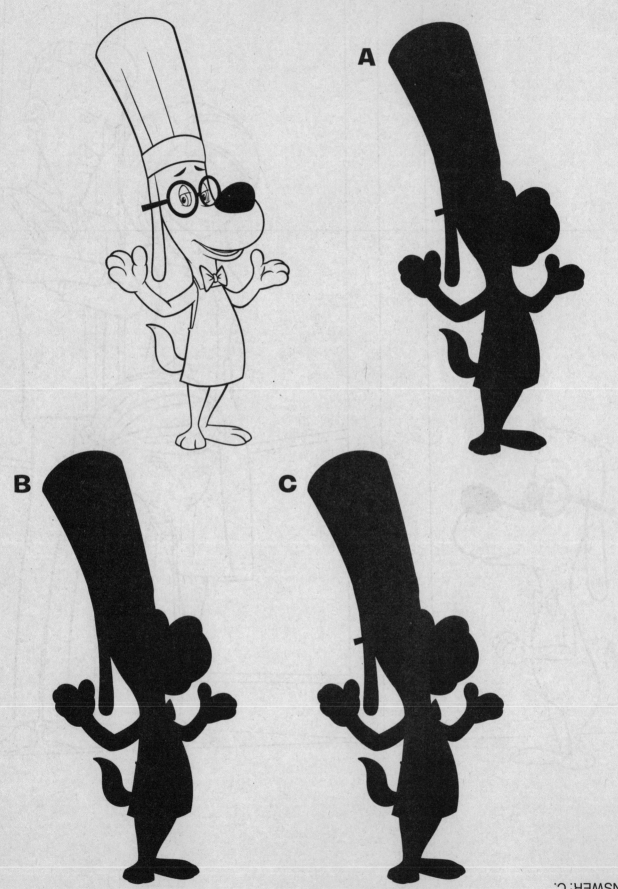

A

B

C

Mr. Peabody is a wonderful chef!

Mr. Peabody entertains his guests
by playing the piano!

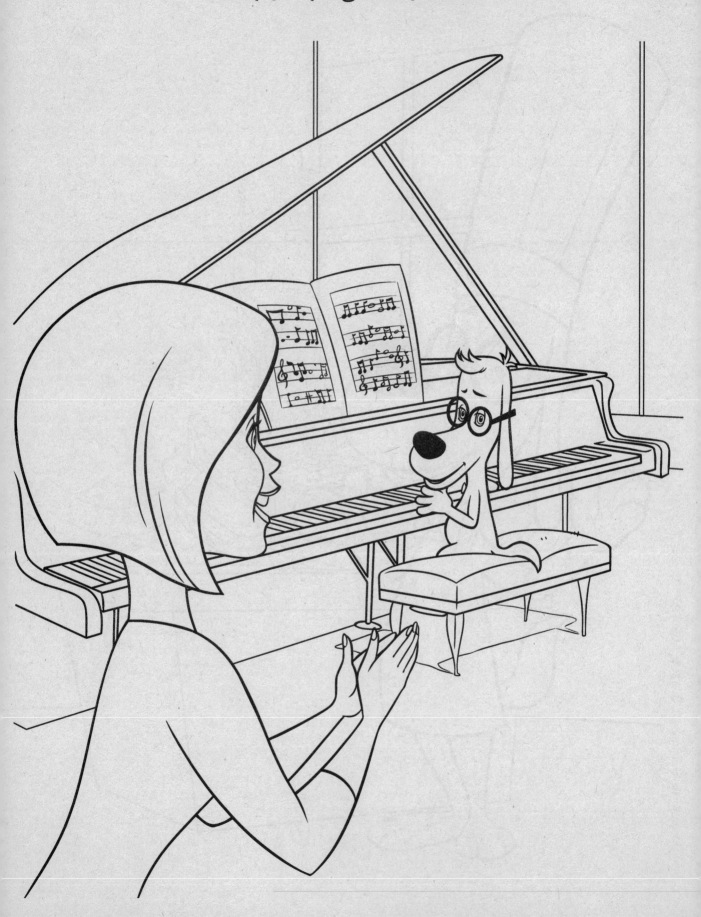

Sherman tells Penny about the WABAC machine. Penny does not believe him.

Sherman shows Penny the WABAC machine.

How many times can you find **WABAC** in the puzzle?
Look up, down, forward, and backward.

A W A B A C W
W A B A C A A
C B A B C B B
W A B A C A A
A C A B A W C

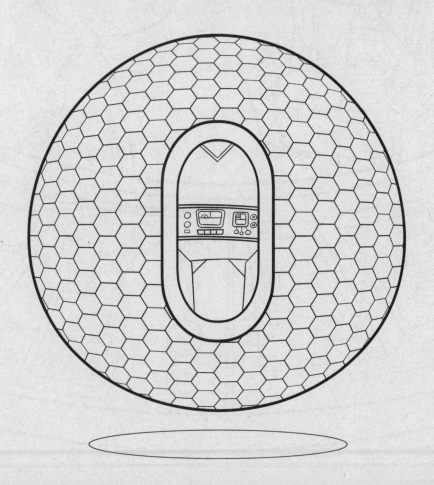

ANSWER: 7.

Oh, no! Penny wants to take
the WABAC machine for a spin.

Where have Sherman and Penny gone?
To find out, follow the lines and write each letter in the correct box.

E N T N T E G C Y P A I

Sherman returns home without Penny!
Mr. Peabody must help Sherman search
for her in the past.

Penny enjoys spending time in ancient Egypt.

King Tut is the ruler of ancient Egypt.

How many times can you find **TUT** in the puzzle?
Look up, down, forward, and backward.

T T U T

T U T U

U T U T

T U T T

ANSWER: 8.

Penny wants to be queen,
so she agrees to marry King Tut!

It's time for the wedding, but Penny doesn't want to marry King Tut anymore.

Mr. Peabody and Sherman need to save Penny!
To find out what they have to do,
put a line through every **X**. Then write
the remaining letters in order on the blanks.

X X S X T X O X X P X T X H X E X
X W X E X X D X D X X I X N X X G

_ _ _ _   _ _ _

_ _ _ _ _ _ _ _ !

Oh, no! King Tut's guards take
Mr. Peabody and Sherman away.

Mr. Peabody finds a way to break out of the tomb!

Mr. Peabody and Sherman use a boat
to make their escape.

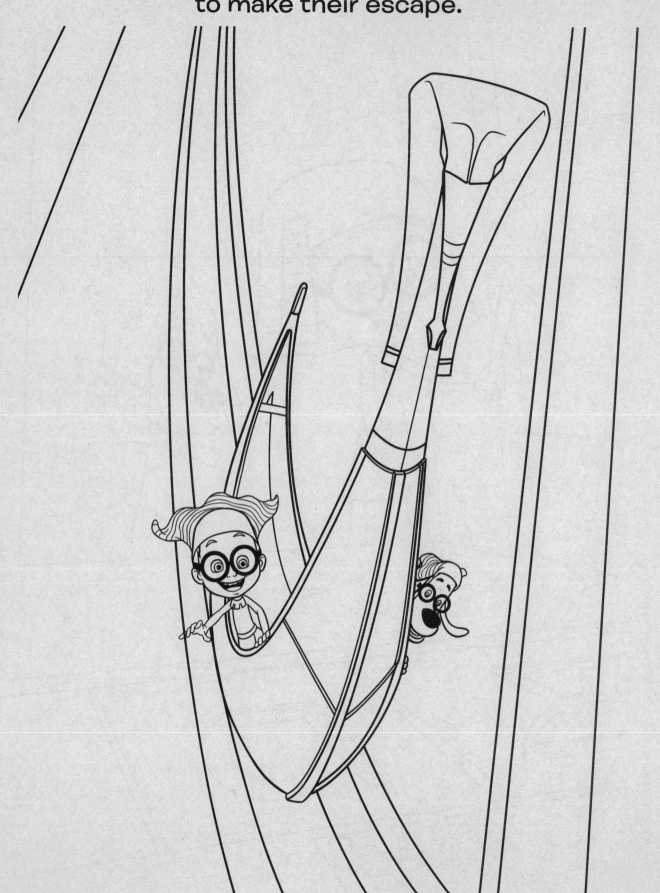

Help Mr. Peabody and Sherman find Penny.

ANSWER:

Mr. Peabody has a plan to stop the wedding!
Sherman helps him.

Mr. Peabody's plan works! They save Penny and zip away before anyone can stop them!

Mr. Peabody, Sherman, and Penny crash into a cart full of oranges!

Which path will lead Mr. Peabody, Sherman, and Penny to the WABAC machine?

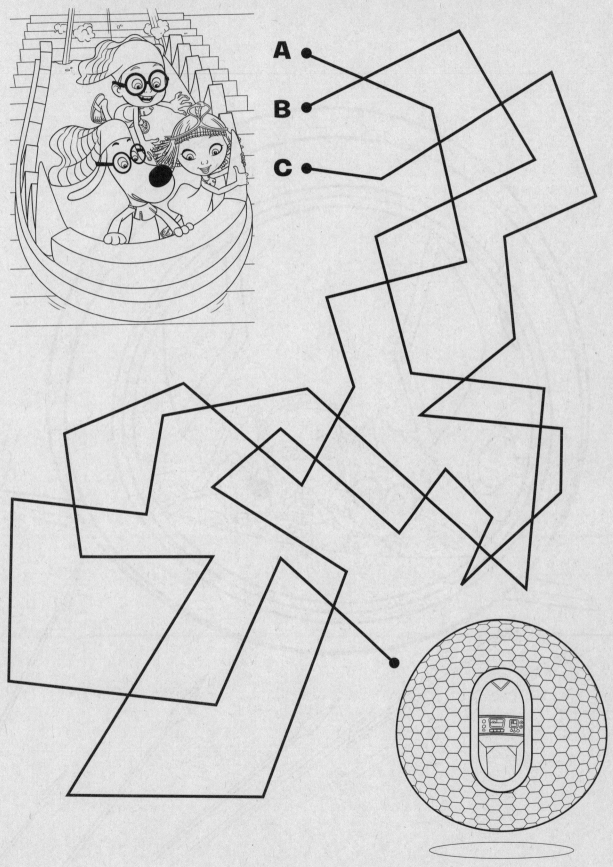

A

B

C

ANSWER: B.

Mr. Peabody fires up the WABAC machine in the nick of time!

As they race through time, the WABAC machine starts to lose power!

Look at the top picture carefully.
Then circle four things that are different in the bottom picture.

ANSWER:

Mr. Peabody has to make a pit stop!
To find out where the WABAC machine lands,
circle every third letter. Then write those
letters in order on the blanks.

SRIHQTWEAMCLFBY

__ __ __ __ __ __

ANSWER: Italy.

Leonardo da Vinci is a famous painter
and inventor from Renaissance Italy.
He is also one of Mr. Peabody's best friends!

Circle the shadow that matches this image of Leonardo da Vinci.

A

B

C

D

ANSWER: B.

Leonardo is working on a painting, but his model won't smile!

Circle the two pictures of the **Mona Lisa** that are exactly the same.

A

B

C

D

ANSWER: A and D.

Oops! Sherman trips and makes a mess of the **Mona Lisa** painting!

Mr. Peabody and Leonardo da Vinci build a machine to power up the WABAC!

Sherman tries to help these
two geniuses—but they are too busy.

Sherman and Penny explore
Leonardo da Vinci's workshop. They even
start to enjoy spending time together!

Penny is curious about Da Vinci's flying machine.
She wants to know how it works.

Sherman and Penny take an unexpected flight!

Yikes! Sherman and Penny crash into a tree!

Mr. Peabody is upset with Sherman
for crashing the flying machine.

Mr. Peabody orders Sherman to sit, but Sherman doesn't listen!

After avoiding a black hole, the WABAC
machine crashes near the ancient city of Troy.
Sherman is nowhere to be found!

Sherman runs away—and joins the Greek army!

Circle the shadow that matches this image of Sherman.

ANSWER: C.

Sherman and the Greek soldiers hide in a wooden horse outside the city of Troy.

The Greek soldiers get ready to attack!

Sherman teaches the soldiers how to high-five!

Mr. Peabody uses an arrow to save
Sherman and Penny!

Sherman and Penny can't find Mr. Peabody!
Now they must figure out a way to return home
and make everything right again.

Sherman comes up with a plan to help Mr. Peabody.

Sherman returns home, but now there are two Shermans and two Mr. Peabodys!

Mr. Peabody and Sherman discover
that their travels through time have
created a hole in the universe!

The past and present are all mixed up!

Sherman tells everyone that Mr. Peabody is the best dad ever!

Mr. Peabody thanks President George
Washington for believing in him.

Mr. Peabody races to the rescue.
Time to fix the hole in the universe!